LITTLE BROWN BEAR
Is Growing Up

Written by Claude Lebrun

Illustrated by Danièle Bour

 Children's Press®

A Division of Grolier Publishing

New York   London   Hong Kong   Sydney

Danbury, Connecticut

Little Brown Bear
is growing up.
In the morning,
he can get down
from his bed
all by himself.

He can get
a banana
and peel it
all by himself.

He can put on
his coat
and button it
all by himself.

When he goes
outside with Papa,
Little Brown Bear
can walk
all by himself.

Little Brown Bear
can open and close
a door
all by himself.

When he is ready
to go to bed,
he can take off
his clothes
all by himself.

Little Brown Bear
is growing up.
He can do things
all by himself.

This series was produced by Mijo Beccaria.

The illustrations were created by Danièle Bour.

The text was written by Claude Lebrun and
edited by Pomme d'Api.

English translation by Children's Press.

Library of Congress Cataloging–in–Publication Data
Lebrun, Claude.
Little Brown Bear is growing up / by Claude Lebrun:
illustrated by Danièle Bour.
p. cm. — (Little Brown Bear books)
Summary: Little Brown Bear takes pride in the things he can do all by himself
including getting down from his bed in the morning and peeling a banana..
ISBN 0-516-07833-X (School & Library Edition)
ISBN 0-516-17833-4 (Trade Edition)
ISBN 0-516-17803-2 (Boxed Set)
[1. Self-reliance — Fiction.] I. Bour, Danièle, ill. II. Title. III. Series: Lebrun, Claude.
Little Brown Bear books.

PZ7.L4698Th
1996[E] — dc20   95-5735
                                                                 CIP
                                                                 AC